Dear mouse friends,
Welcome to the world of

Geronimo Stilton

THE RODENT'S GAZETTE
EDITORIAL STAFF

Geronimo Stilton
A learned and brainy
mouse; editor of
The Rodent's Gazette

Thea Stilton
Geronimo's sister and
special correspondent at
The Rodent's Gazette

Trap Stilton
An awful joker;
Geronimo's cousin and
owner of the store
Cheap Junk for Less

Benjamin Stilton
A sweet and loving
nine-year-old mouse;
Geronimo's favorite
nephew

Geronimo Stilton

GERONIMO STILTON, SECRET AGENT

Scholastic Inc.

New York   Toronto   London   Auckland   Sydney
Mexico City   New Delhi   Hong Kong   Buenos Aires

No part of this publication may be reproduced, stored in a retrieval system, or transmitted in any form or by any means, electronic, mechanical, photocopying, recording, or otherwise, without written permission from the copyright holder. For information regarding permission, please contact: Atlantyca S.p.A., Via Leopardi 8, 20123 Milan, Italy; e-mail foreignrights@atlantyca.it, www.atlantyca.com.

ISBN 978-0-545-02134-0

Copyright © 2007 by Edizioni Piemme S.p.A., Via Tiziano 32, 20145 Milan, Italy.

International Rights © Atlantyca S.p.A.

English translation © 2008 by Atlantyca S.p.A.

GERONIMO STILTON names, characters, and related indicia are copyright, trademark, and exclusive license of Atlantyca S.p.A. All rights reserved. The moral right of the author has been asserted.

Based on an original idea by Elisabetta Dami.

www.geronimostilton.com

Published by Scholastic Inc., 557 Broadway, New York, NY 10012. SCHOLASTIC and associated logos are trademarks and/or registered trademarks of Scholastic Inc.

Stilton is the name of a famous English cheese. It is a registered trademark of the Stilton Cheese Makers' Association. For more information, go to www.stiltoncheese.com

Text by Geronimo Stilton
Original title *Agente segreto zero zero kappa*
Cover by Cleo Bianca and Christian Aliprandi
Illustrations by Cleo Bianca and Christian Aliprandi
Graphics by Merenguita Gingermouse and Sara Baruffaldi

Special thanks to Kathryn Cristaldi
Translated by Lidia Morson Tramontozzi
Interior design by Kay Petronio

30 29 28 27 26 25 24 23 22 21   12 13 14 15 16/0

Printed in the U.S.A.   40
First printing, July 2008

A Suspicious-Looking Rodent . . .

That morning was just like any other morning. I woke up and smelled the cheese — hot cheddar, that is. I like to make a whole pot every day.

Then I stuffed my paws into my comfy CAT-FUR SLIPPERS. I shuffled to the window to check the weather. The forecast was for rain. But when I looked outside, I just saw lots of

CLOUDS. Clouds, and **A VERY SUSPICIOUS-LOOKING RODENT WITH DARK SUNGLASSES ACROSS THE STREET.** How odd.

I took a shower and gobbled down my breakfast — melted cheddar toast. Yum! Then I headed for the subway. I was humming one of my favorite love songs, "Beady-eyed Beauty," when I saw him again. **THAT SAME SUSPICIOUS-LOOKING RODENT WITH THE**

SUNGLASSES WAS WALKING RIGHT BEHIND ME. How strange.

A few minutes later, I arrived at my stop. I scampered out the door. GUESS WHO WAS RIGHT ON MY TAIL? YOU GOT IT. MR. DARK SUNGLASSES. How very odd!

At last, I reached my office at 17 Swiss Cheese Place. I couldn't believe it. **MR. SUNGLASSES HAD BEATEN ME THERE. I WAS STARTING TO GET A LITTLE CREEPED OUT. A CHILL RAN DOWN MY FUR. WHAT DID HE WANT FROM ME?** Why was he following me?

Part of me was afraid to find out. What if he mistook me for an escaped con rat? What if I reminded him of someone he didn't like? What if he hated my tie? I decided there was only one thing left to do. I raced up the stairs to my office and **slammed** the door. Then I buried my snout in work.

But when I looked out the window at lunchtime, guess who I saw? **YEP, IT WAS THAT MOUSE AGAIN!**

He was **THERE** when I left the office. He was **THERE** when I reached my house. He was **THERE** after I **scarfed down** a super-size three-cheese pizza for dinner.

Finally, I couldn't take it anymore. I just had to find out who that mouse was. With a squeak, I yanked open the door to my house. Then I stuck out my snout and yelled,

"WHO ARE YOU AND WHAT DO YOU WANT FROM ME?"

DON'T YOU RECOGNIZE ME?

Even though I was screaming at the top of my lungs, the rodent **barely flinched.** Instead he calmly took off his *sunglasses* and *SMILED.*

Or was it a smirk?

How strange! The rodent looked so familiar. Was it the **trench coat**? Was it the paws in the pockets? Was it the perfectly *groomed* fur?

I touched a paw to my own head. Hmmm . . . my fur was getting a little long. I made a mental note to make an appointment at Clip Rat's Salon and Day Spa.

I was still thinking about furcuts when the rodent suddenly **tapped** me on the forehead. He stared into my eyes.

Cheese nibblets! Was he trying to hypnotize me? I **gulped**. I'd read about bad mice like this. First they put you under a spell. Then they break into your mouse hole and steal all your MONEY!

The rodent's beady eyes seemed to drill right into me. I was so nervous I could barely see straight. I tried practicing the deep-breathing techniques I had learned in Penny Pretzel Paws's yoga class. They didn't work. I guess I wasn't paying enough attention in class.

Just then, the rodent leaned in closer. I BROKE OUT in a cold sweat. *This is it,* I mumbled to myself. *Good-bye, Mouse World.*

But instead of hypnotizing me, the rodent snickered.

"Don't you RECOGNIZE me, Geronimo?" he said.

"IT'S KORNELIUS VON KICKPAW."

I could hardly believe my eyes. The last time I'd seen **KORNELIUS**, I was still learning how to do math and tie my shoes. We were friends in *elementary school*!

A Mouse Wearing a Trench Coat

In school, **KORNELIUS** sat in the desk behind me. He **ALWAYS** wore a trench coat no matter what the weather was like. And he **ALWAYS** wore dark **SUNGLASSES** even when it wasn't sunny!

Yes, he was an **odd** sort of mouse, but we were **good friends** anyway. One time, Wendell Wild Whiskers and his gang stuffed me into a gym locker. **KORNELIUS** came to my rescue. He ripped open the locker and made Wendell apologize. After that, the bullies **NEVER** picked on me again. I always felt safe when **KORNELIUS** was around.

I *smiled* thinking about those days. Even though we hadn't squeaked in years, **KORNELIUS** would always be a great friend.

Do you have any friends like **KORNELIUS**? If you do, you are very lucky. As my dear aunt Sweetfur likes to say,

"Whoever finds a friend... finds a treasure!"

I invited Kornelius into my house. Then I showed him around. It didn't take very long.

My mouse hole isn't very big. Still, I'm super proud of it. I especially love my kitchen with my megahuge fridge.

While we were in the kitchen, I whipped up some tasty grilled cheese sandwiches. **KORNELIUS** munched them down in two seconds flat! Did I mention he's a **big** mouse?

Finally, we sat down in my living room to chat. We had so much catching up to do. We squeaked about old times, old friends, and my job at *The Rodent's Gazette*.

"So what kind of work do you do, Kornelius?" I asked.

My friend held up his paw.

"It's **TOP SECRET**," he whispered. "You have to promise you won't tell anyone."

I gasped. Why was my friend being so mysterious? Was he a professional burglar? Was he in the witmouse-protection program?

 "I **promise**," I agreed, eyes wide.

KORNELIUS put his paw around my shoulder. Then he leaned in close and whispered.

 "My code name is **OOK**. I'm a **SECRET AGENT**."

THE VON KICKPAW ESTATE

I was convinced **KORNELIUS** was pulling my paw. I mean, I'd seen secret agents before in the movies, but not in New Mouse City.

"I'm not acting, Geronimo," my friend insisted. He **DROVE** me to his mansion in the country. On the way there, Kornelius explained that he was involved with **SECRET MISSIONS** for the government of Mouse Island. I felt like I was in a dream.

At last, we reached the **MANSION**. **What a sight!**

I knew my friend was rich, but this place was more spectacular than Elvis Mousely's estate! The property was surrounded by a

1. Mansion
2. Greenhouse for rare plants
3. Tennis court
4. Helicopter pad
5. Garage
6. Swimming pool
7. Stable and paddock for horses
8. Private beach and yacht
9. Golf course

gleaming wrought-iron gate with the letters VK inscribed at the entrance. The driveway wound its way past a *perfectly manicured lawn*. I spotted a greenhouse, tennis courts, and a stable for horses.

The inside of the mansion was almost as amazing as the outside. The entryway was made of white marble. Two MAGNIFICENT gold and diamond-studded chandeliers GLIMMERED over our heads. And there was even a fountain shaped like a gigantic wedge of cheese in the hallway. Kornelius ushered me into the living room. It was filled with *priceless* antiques. Paintings by famouse artists decorated the walls. I stared at a painting of a gorgeous rodent hanging above the fireplace.

Wow, what a STUNNING mouse! I couldn't take my eyes off her.

"That's my sister, *Veronica*," said Kornelius. "She's a secret agent, too. Her code name is 00V."

Just then, I sensed something behind me. When I turned around, my jaw dropped. **It was her!** It was **00V**! My heart began racing like a car at the Indy Mouse 500. Did I mention I get a little nervous around beautiful rodents?

"Is that you on the wall? Uh, er, in the frame? I mean, in the painting?" I babbled.

The rodent flashed me a tiny smile. Or was it a smirk? Then she vanished. A *delicate* perfume lingered in the room.

Wow, what a *stunning* mouse!

I wondered if I could ask her out for a cup of hot cheddar sometime. Too bad she disappeared so quickly.

I was still **dreaming** about 00V when **KORNELIUS** led me into the library. We sat down on two **comfy** leather pawchairs.

Without a word, Kornelius patted the arm of his chair. Seconds later, the rug slid aside. We were sitting on top of a trapdoor! Before I could let out a squeak, I found myself zipping down a **Steep, Dark Tunnel.**

"Tell me when it's over!" I cried.

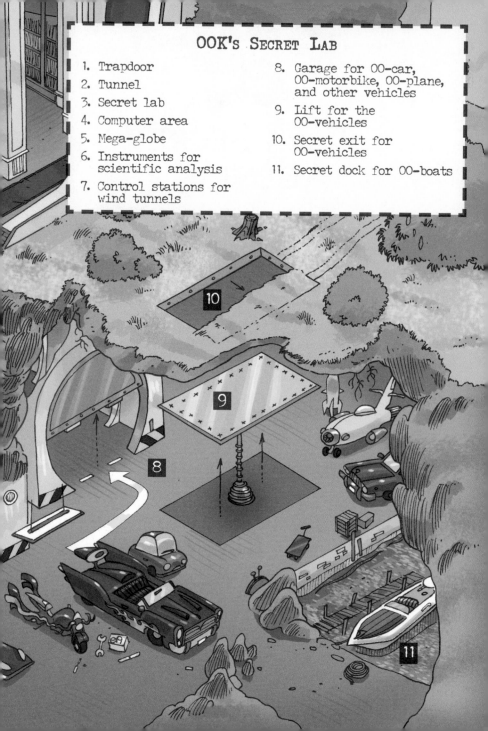

OOK's Secret Lab

1. Trapdoor
2. Tunnel
3. Secret lab
4. Computer area
5. Mega-globe
6. Instruments for scientific analysis
7. Control stations for wind tunnels

8. Garage for OO-car, OO-motorbike, OO-plane, and other vehicles
9. Lift for the OO-vehicles
10. Secret exit for OO-vehicles
11. Secret dock for OO-boats

I'M A SECRET
AGENT . . .

Minutes later, we landed in an *elegant* living room. We were still seated in our **PAWCHAIRS**, but now we were underground in a very **MYSTERIOUS** place.

I pinched myself to make sure I wasn't dreaming. Youch! That hurt! I may not be a tough mouse, but I do have one painful pinch.

After I recovered, Kornelius, aka **OOK**, showed me all of his agent gear. This included a *bow tie* that turned into a rope, a ring filled with **sneEzing** powder, and antigravity shoes.

I was impressed and a little bit scared. Just then, Kornelius looked at me with a piercing

am3e8v3759fjdlafvmdhfoq45677xdqifphlktnru3945g
lktnru724...
am...
lkt...
am...

OOK

NAME: Kornelius von Kickpaw

CODE NAME: OOK

PROFESSION: Secret Agent

WHO IS HE: Geronimo's friend from elementary school.

PECULIARITIES: Always wears a trench coat and sunglasses, even at night!

am3e8v3759fjdlafvmdhfoq45677xdqifphlktnru3945g

ryr9dMTPSsmaeroasjetietvu9654seu49g0wtbtdow'3955
jeti9g0...'7)55 fx adhfcq45677x
ryr9d...5
jeti9g...'x
ryr9d...55
jeti9g...7x
ryr90...55

OOV

NAME: Veronica
von Kickpaw

CODE NAME: OOV

PROFESSION: Secret
Agent

WHO IS SHE:
Kornelius's sister

PECULIARITIES:
Always wears a
mysterious, delicate,
and sophisticated
perfume that makes
her immediately identifiable and . . .
fascinating!

jeti9...7x
ryr9...955
jeti9...77x
ryr9...955
jeti9...77x
ryr...5955
jeti...577x
ryr...3955
eti...677x
cyr...'3955
et...5677x
ry...'3955
et...5677x
cy...w'3955
etiyyow...5677x
ryr9dMTPSsmaeroasjetietvu9654seu49gow...w'3955

stare. I gulped. Had I done something wrong already?

"Let me tell you why you're here," Kornelius began. He opened a little **black** case and took out a stack of newspapers.

To my surprise, the articles were all about me. There was even a **color** photo of me in front of *The Rodent's Gazette*. I have to admit it wasn't a very good one. "**Are my ears really that big**?" I muttered.

KORNELIUS shook his head. "Forget about your ears, Geronimo; you have more important things to worry about," he advised. "By reading the paper, anybody can figure out where you live, where you work, where you go on vacation, who your friends are. Your life's one open book!"

"This is dangerous, Geronimo," he continued. "If an **EVIL** rodent wanted to hurt you or play a mean trick on you, they would have no problem. It would be like **taking cheese** from a young mouselet. You need someone to protect you. And I'm here to say, **I'M YOUR MOUSE.**"

I felt flattered. I mean, it's not often that you have a **SECRET AGENT** friend who wants to be your own furry **BODYGUARD**. Still, I politely declined.

Kornelius tried to make a list of all the things that could get me in trouble, and when it was time to leave, Kornelius made me **PROMISE** I would call him if I ever got into any trouble.

I grinned.

Aunt Sweetfur sure was right. A friend is a true treasure.

WHAT A GREAT DAY!

The next morning, I woke up feeling extra happy. I had good friends, a good family, and a great life. I gobbled down my breakfast and practically skipped out my door. A strong wind was **BLOWING**, but I wasn't going to let that get me down. I smiled, thinking about how I used to love flying kites when I was a tiny mouselet. The sun was shining so I decided to walk to work.

What a great day!

While I was walking, I thought about my friend Kornelius. He really didn't need to worry about me. Today, I was feeling more than double okay!

The wind was **BLOWING** hard when I reached my office. I shut the door behind me and **RACED** upstairs.

"Geronimo, don't forget that today there is an important meeting with the president of the New Mouse City Historical Society and your grandfather," Priscilla Prettywhiskers reminded me.

Do you know Priscilla? She's one of the

editors at *The Rodent's Gazette.*

Now I looked at her and **frowned**.

"**MEETING**?" I mumbled. "What **MEETING**?"

Priscilla reminded me that the head of the historical society was coming to check out *The Rodent's Gazette.* It seems they were doing research on the **oldest** buildings in the city. The *Gazette* was on the list.

Rats!

HOW COULD I FORGET SUCH AN IMPORTANT MEETING?

I threw open the door to my office. I had to get my notes ready for the meeting. If I wasn't prepared, Grandfather would have my tail!

I was so worried about Grandfather that, at first, I didn't notice anything different. Then it hit me. A **cold** gust of **WIND** sent my whiskers whirling. **Cheese nibblets!** The night before I had accidentally left MY WINDOW WIDE OPEN!

I watched in horror as the fierce **WIND** picked up a large envelope with a **red seal**. The gust lifted the envelope off my desk and blew it straight out the window. With a *squeak*, I tried catching it, but I was too late. My snout **smacked** down hard on my desk. Youch! I wondered if I'd ever be able to sniff again.

VERY VERY IMPORTANT
ENVELOPE PUT ON
GERONIMO'S DESK
BY PRISCILLA

The Rodent's Gazette

As I **rubbed** my nose, I told myself not to panic. After all, as the publisher of a newspaper, I was always getting tons of **nutty mail**. That envelope was probably from some wacky mouse wanting me to do a story on alien cats or something.

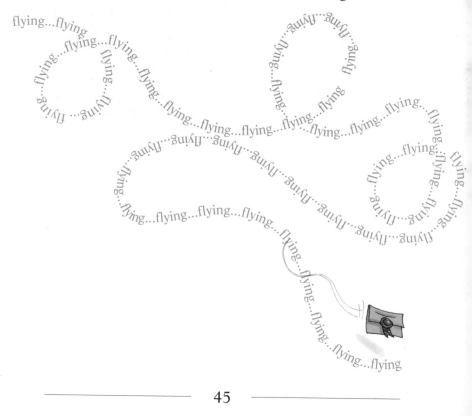

I THINK I LOST IT

At that moment, the door to my office burst open.

"GRAN**DSON**! The meeting has already started! What are you doing in here?!" a gruff mouse shrieked.

I gulped. It was my highly stressed, highly irritable, highly **DEMANDING** grandfather, William Shortpaws.

A shiver ran down my fur.

"The meeting has STARTED. You're **LATE, LATE, LATE**, with a capital **L**!" he screamed. "The president of the *New Mouse City Historical Society* and the committee members are waiting for us. Let's move it. And, Grandson, try not to **EMBARRASS** me. Got it?"

We sat at our usual seats in the conference room.

Richard F. Ramblesnout, the head of the historical society, cleared his throat.

"Ahem, welcome, gentlemice. Let's get started. I'll be **BRIEF** ..." he began.

I chewed my whiskers. Whenever anyone starts with, "I'll be brief," they usually end up squeaking on and on forever. In fact, that's exactly what happened.

After a little while, I began to doze off.

I was awakened by a piercing **SHOUT**.

"**GRANDSON**!" yelled my grandfather. "Are you **sleeping**?"

My fur turned **red** with **embarrassment**.

"Did you hear what Mr. Ramblesnout said?" he shrieked. "There is an **INCREDIBLY RARE** and valuable document on your desk.

It's in a large envelope with a **red seal** on it. Go get it. Now!"

I couldn't move. I couldn't breathe. I couldn't think. How could this be happening? That envelope with the **red seal** on it was no junk mail. It was valuable. VERY VALUABLE!

"Um, well, unfortunately, I, um, think I lost it," I whispered softly.

Grandfather threw a fit.

"**What?!** Get that wax out of your ears and listen up. I want that document here, on this table, by nine o'clock tomorrow morning! **GOT IT**?" he shouted.

disbelief

shock

astonishment

Everybody turned to **LOOK AT ME**.

I FELT FAINT.

I saw in their eyes: **disbelief**, **shock**, **ASTONISHMENT**,

bewilderment

bewilderment, **BAFFLEMENT**, **ANNOYANCE**, **INDIGNATION**, **ANGER**, sympathy, and **PITY**.

bafflement

What could I do? What could I say? I had to find that envelope. I just had to!

"I'll do my best," I coughed.

annoyance

Then I slunk out of the room with **MY TAIL BETWEEN MY LEGS**.

indignation

pity

sympathy

anger

A VOLCANO
READY TO EXPLODE

I got back to my office and collapsed behind my desk. Oh, how did I get myself into such a mess? I stared out the window. I could hear the wind roaring. It looked like a storm was brewing.

A few minutes later, **Grandfather William** scampered into my office.

He didn't slam the door. **Odd**.

He didn't yell. Even more **Odd**.

I braced myself. Talk about a storm **BREWING**. I knew Grandfather William too well. When he was angry, he was like a **VOLCANO** ready to **explode**. Like a water balloon ready to **pop**. Like a pan of cheese popcorn ready to **burst**. Hmm . . . cheese popcorn . . . My stomach began to growl. I was hungry for my midmorning cheddar muffin. But it would have to wait.

"Geronimo, do you have any idea what's inside that envelope?" he began.

I started to answer, but he interrupted me.

"It's the **DEED** to this land!" he **thundered**. "It's the only proof we have that we own the property. If some rotten mouse gets his or her paws on that envelope, we'll lose *The Rodent's Gazette*!"

I closed my eyes. Oh, how did I get myself into such a mess?

I'm not sure I want to know!

HOW HARD
COULD IT BE?

After Grandfather **STORMED** out of my office, I had a terrible **NIGHTMARE**. Well, it wasn't exactly a nightmare since it was only 11:30 in the morning, but you get the idea. A **HORRIFYING** picture of Sally Ratmousen flashed before my eyes. She was waving an envelope with a **red seal** screaming,

"The Rodent's Gazette is mine, mine, mine!"

I FELT AWFUL. Like I had just lost everything: the newspaper, my job, my appetite. Well, maybe not that last one. After all, it was nearly lunchtime.

Just then, I noticed a PHOTO of me on my desk. It was a shot of me CLIMBING Mouse Everest.

Suddenly, I felt a surge of **energy**. If I could climb a mountain as high as **Mouse Everest**, how hard could it be to find a silly old envelope?

By now, it was noon. I needed to find the envelope by **nine** A.M. the next morning. That meant I still had twenty-one hours.

I grabbed a *pen and paper* and sat down to make a list. I love making lists. They help me to stay

ORGANIZED. I wrote down all of the things I needed to do:

1. Be calm.
2. Ask friends for help.
3. Call the weather mouse to find out the speed and direction of the wind.
4. Trace a possible route on a map of New Mouse City that the envelope might have taken.
5. Get going!
IMPORTANT!
Remember to take a supply of Cheesy Chews!

I began to do the things written on my list:

1. Be CALM.

Then I called my sister, Thea. The answering machine picked up.

"I'm not at home. Leave a message. *Beep!*"

I called my cousin Trap. His answering machine picked up, too.

"I'm not home. Or if I am, I'm busy eating. I mean, cooking. I mean **eating and cooking**. Leave a message. *Beep!*"

I thought about calling my friend Petunia Pretty Paws. She's so smart and beautiful. But I was too embarrassed. I didn't want Petunia to think I was a complete *furbrain* for losing such an important document. Instead, I tried my friend Burt Burlyrat. We had met at a survival camp in the **jungle**.

I got his answering machine. "I'm not in, but you might be able to find me in the AMAZON. That is, *if you don't mind a few hungry pythons and some killer quicksand. Beep!*"

WHY, OH, WHY, WAS NO ONE HOME WHEN YOU NEEDED THEM?

For a nanosecond, I thought of **OOK**.

But just like with Petunia, I was too embarrassed. Besides, I had already told Kornelius I didn't need his help.

"**ALL RIGHT, DON'T PANIC**," I said out loud, trying to give myself a pep talk. "This means you will have no help. You will be all *ALONE*. And you will have to do everything by yourself."

I put my head in my paws. Then I began sobbing uncontrollably.

Guess my pep talk needed work. Lots of work.

I'M YOUR BIGGEST FAN!

After I stopped **crying**, I wrung out my *whiskers*. Then I looked at my list again.

I skipped over number **ONE** (Be **calm**), skipped number **TWO** (Ask **friends** for help), and went straight to numbers **THREE** and **FOUR**. First I found a map of New Mouse City. I spread it out across my desk. Next I dialed the number for the local **weather center**.

1. Be calm.
2. Ask friends for help.
3. Call the weather mouse to find out the speed and direction of the wind.
4. Trace a possible route on a map of New Mouse City that the envelope might have taken.
5. Get going!
IMPORTANT!
Remember to take a supply of Cheesy Chews!

"Ahem, good morning. My name is Stilton, *Geronimo Stilton*. I need some information on the speed and direction of the wind in New Mouse City from around nine o'clock to twelve o'clock . . ." I began.

I was greeted by an excited squeak.

"oh, Mr. Stilton! What an honor!

I am your biggest fan! I've read all of your books!" a female rodent gushed. "Why do you need to know about the *WIND*? Are you writing a book about it? Are you coming down to the weather center? Oh, I'm so excited. I would love to meet you. Maybe we can chat. Or do lunch. Or how about a movie?"

I blushed. Sometimes I'm a little shy around my female fans.

"Um, well, I don't have time to come there today," I explained. "I really just need to know the direction of the wind."

"Of course, of course," the mouse agreed. Then she told me the **awful news**. It seemed the wind had done something **really strange** this morning. It had changed direction every fifteen minutes! She **FiRED OFF** a list of speeds and times.

By the time I got off the phone, my left ear was on **FIRE**, my paw was **cramped**, and I had made a date to go see *The Return of Catzilla*.

Oh, why could I never say  to my female fans?

Here's the route the envelope took

The Rodent's Gazette

HOW EMBARRASSING!

Just then, I glanced at the clock. Cheese nibblets! It was already two-thirty. There was no time to waste.

I SKIPPED straight to number FIVE on my list: Get going!  With a squeak, I SCURRIED outside as fast as my paws would carry me.

I decided to CHECK OUT New Mouse City's port. It's a very busy place. It's where all of the big boats enter the city dock. Plus, there are tons of vendors selling fresh fish, fruits, and vegetables.

By the time I reached the port, my paws were THROBBING. Did I mention I'm

not a very athletic mouse? Still, there was no time to rest. I had to find that envelope! I scoured every **fishing boat**. I patted down every fishing net. I even peered in the open mouths of one hundred slimy tuna fish.

What a stench! I could barely breathe. But I had to keep going.

Then I spotted a row of **garbage cans**. Each one was filled with rotting, smelly fish bones.

What could I do? With a groan, I stuck my snout inside the first **GARBAGE CAN**.

I didn't notice a woman staring at me.

"Aren't you *Geronimo Stilton*?" she said, wrinkling her nose.

It was Petunia Pretty Paws's aunt. HOW EMBARRASSING!

A few minutes later, a very old mouse with a cane strolled by.

"Aren't you *Geronimo Stilton*?" he said, shaking his head.

It was my grandfather's old friend Sniffty. HOW EMBARRASSING!

I stuck my snout deeper into the next garbage can, trying to hide. But a pretty young rodent spotted me.

"Aren't you *Geronimo Stilton*?" she said, looking shocked.

It was Benjamin's schoolteacher. HOW EMBARRASSING!

I had made a fool of myself. And I hadn't even found the envelope! Two minutes later, a seagull swooped down and pooped right on my head. What next?

ON TOP OF A STINKY MOUNTAIN

I sat on the sidewalk totally DEPRESSED. Just then, I heard a loud GRUMBLING. My fur stood on end. Was it a killer whale? Was it a ferocious sea monster? Was this how it would all end? Headlines flashed through my brain: CRAZED WHALE GRABS STILTON BY THE TAIL! STILTON SUCKED UP BY SEA CREATURE!

Then I realized the **grumbling** was coming from my tummy. I WAS starved!

Too bad, I had forgotten the most important thing on my list: a supply of Cheesy Chews.

1. Be calm.
2. Ask friends for help.
3. Call the weather mouse to find out the speed and direction of the wind.
4. Trace a possible route on a map of New Mouse City that the envelope might have taken.
5. Get going!

IMPORTANT!
Remember to take a supply of Cheesy Chews!

I stared at the **smelly** garbage cans feeling even more depressed. And that's when it hit me. No, not more seagull poop. This time, it was an idea.

Where could I find all the garbage in New Mouse City? At the town dump, of course! If the envelope had fallen on the ground, it would surely have been swept up. Then it would go straight to the **dump**!

Before throwing anything away, do you ever ask yourself if somebody else could use it, or if it could be recycled, that is, used again?

Certain types of garbage, such as **paper, plastic, glass,** and **aluminum** are recyclable and can be used to produce new things. By recycling, we save natural resources and the energy that is needed to make new products.

Separating the recyclables
If we learn to divide garbage according to its composition and place it in assigned containers, the paper, plastic, glass, and aluminum can be recycled.

In New Mouse City:

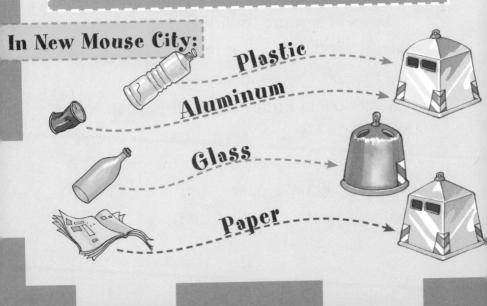

Plastic

Aluminum

Glass

Paper

Where does garbage end up?

Recycling Plants
There are recycling centers that collect various types of garbage, such as paper, glass, plastic, and aluminum, rework it, and then reuse it.

Garbage Dumps
All garbage that is not recyclable ends up in garbage dumps.

Incinerators
There are plants where garbage is burned to eliminate it. As the refuse is burned, a tremendous amount of heat is released, which can then be transformed into energy.

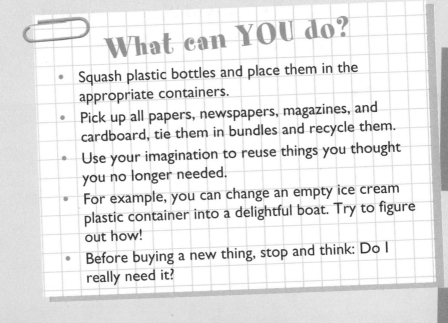

What can YOU do?

- Squash plastic bottles and place them in the appropriate containers.
- Pick up all papers, newspapers, magazines, and cardboard, tie them in bundles and recycle them.
- Use your imagination to reuse things you thought you no longer needed.
- For example, you can change an empty ice cream plastic container into a delightful boat. Try to figure out how!
- Before buying a new thing, stop and think: Do I really need it?

Right at that moment, a GARBAGE truck rumbled by. *I TOOK OFF LIKE LIGHTNING. LIKE A ROCKET. LIKE THE WORLD'S FASTEST MARATHON MOUSE.* Well, okay, maybe I wasn't that fast. In fact, I was pretty slow. But don't tell anyone.

Before long, I reached the garbage dump. **WHAT A SIGHT!** The garbage was piled up a mile high. And it **smelLed** worse than my cousin Rancid Rat's stinky breath. I climbed on top of a huge pile and rested.

GARBAGE, MORE GARBAGE, AND . . . EVEN MORE GARBAGE!

Just then, a truck arrived. And before I could squeak, it happened. A whole mound of new GARBAGE came pouring out of the truck. It all crashed down right on top of me! I began rolling down the hill like an out of control furball. Oh, what a mess I was in this time. **AND I MEAN MESS!** I tried to grab hold of something, but all I got was a rotten banana peel. "**Help**! I screeched.

"I'M BEING BURIED ALIVE IN JUNK!"

I moved my arms through the garbage as if I were swimming to keep myself from being buried alive.

Suddenly, I felt two strong paws PULLING me out of the garbage heap.

"I'm here to help," a deep voice said. At the same time, I smelled a delicate perfume.

Hmm . . . it seemed so familiar.

"Thanks," I mumbled before I PASSED OUT.

When I came to, I was still at the town dump, but I wasn't rolling anymore. I looked around. I was alone.

Who had saved me?

And why did he disappear? It was a real MYSTERY.

Who had saved me and why?

I was still thinking about my MYSTERIOUS rescuer when I noticed the wind had picked up. THOUSANDS of pieces of paper began swirling all around me.

At that moment, I spotted an envelope drifting right above my head.

Could it be? It was! It was the envelope with the **red seal** — the one I'd been searching for!

But just as I *reached* to grab it,

it Disappeared Down a Mouse Hole Cover.

DOWN, DOWN, DOWN, INTO A SEA OF FOUL SLIME!

What could I do? I **had** to get that envelope.

With a **GROAN**, I lifted up the grate and lowered myself into the mouse hole. It was **DARK**. So very dark. My teeth began to **CHATTER**. Did I mention I'm afraid of the

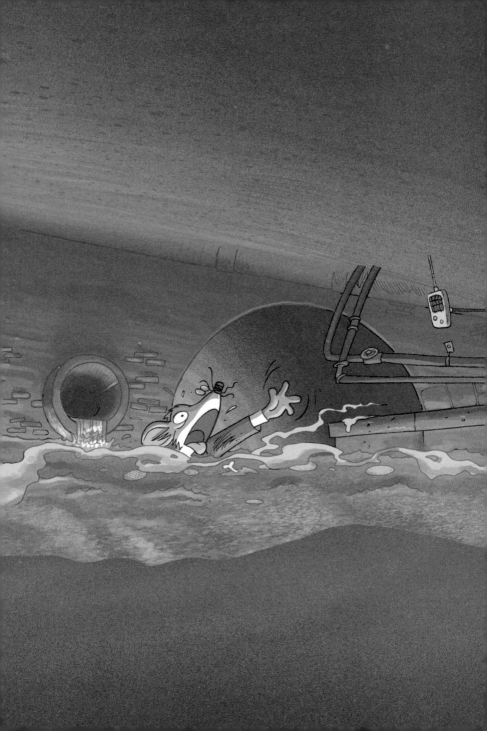

dark and tight spaces and the ding of the toaster oven? Oh, but that's another story for another time. I was wishing I had worn the glow-in-the-dark tie my cousin Trap had given me so I could see a little better. Just then, I slipped.

Down, down, down I tumbled snoutfirst into the darkness.

After what seemed like a million years, I landed with a sickening splash. I found myself floating in a sea of slimy grEEn liquid. The smell was worse than the town dump. Welcome to the sewers of New Mouse City.

I dragged myself out of the water and looked around. No sign of the envelope with the **red seal**.

But I did see something. Something shiny and YELLOW. I blinked. A pair of

GLITTERING eyes stared at me through the darkness.

My whiskers began to tremble. Who in their right mind would live down here in the sewer?

Just then, the creature cackled softly. Ha, ha, ha. Was it laughing at me? Was it going to POUNCE on me? Was this how it would all end?

I braced myself for an ATTACK, but nothing happened. Instead, the YELLOW eyes

took off into the darkness. At first, I was glad to see them go. Then I was even more scared. Without those eyes, the sewer was darker than theater four at the Cheddarville Tenplex. There was only one thing left to do. Follow those eyes.

I **CHASED** them the entire night. I was exhausted. Finally, they stopped, turned around, and started chasing me!

RANCID RAT HAIRS! Now what was I supposed to do?

"Ha, ha, ha," the creature cackled.

This was it. I was a GONER. Oh why hadn't I let my friend **KORNELIUS** help me? He was right. I was no good at protecting myself. I was always getting myself into these jams. I mean, the last time I tried to bake cookies I got my tail stuck in the oven. My burning fur set off the smoke alarm.

I was so embarrassed when the firemice showed up on my doorstep.

"HELP! HELP! Somebody help me!" I squeaked at the top of my lungs.

Meanwhile the yellow eyes zoomed closer.

Suddenly, I realized who they belonged to: an enormous crocodile! And even worse, it was holding the envelope with the red seal in its ferocious jaws! Cheese

nibblets! I closed my eyes and wished for a miracle. I could hear the **crocodile** gnashing its teeth. Its breath smelled like **rotten** goat cheese. Hadn't this guy heard about the dangers of tooth decay?

I was still thinking about teeth when someone **GRABBED** me by the shoulder.

"I'm here to help," a familiar voice said. Again, I smelled a *delicate* perfume.

I opened my eyes, but it was too dark. I

could only see the eyes of the crocodile. They were staring right at me. The croc looked hungry. Very hungry.

"Good-bye, Mouse World," I sobbed. Then **I FAINTED**.

When I came to, I was back on the street. It was already dawn.

I looked all around me but didn't see anyone.

Who had saved me?

Why did he *disappear*?

It was a real MYSTERY.

Who had saved me and why?

Up, Up, Up ... into Sally Ratmousen's Office

I sat on the curb feeling totally confused.
What had just happened to me?
How did I get out of the sewer?
Who was my mysterious rescuer?

But above all, what happened to the envelope with the **red seal** that was between the **crocodile's** teeth?

Do you know what happened next? A miracle. A real miracle. I looked up and there it was — the envelope! The wind had picked it up and carried it high above my head.

iT FLEW HiGHER AND HiGHER.

An instant later, it slipped into an open window.

DOUBLE-twiStED RAttAïLS! That window belonged to my biggest enemy, Sally Ratmousen. Do you know Sally? She is the owner of *The Daily Rat*. Her dream is to put *The Rodent's Gazette* out of business.

Now what was I supposed to do? Sally would never let me into her office. Firstly, I was covered in stinky, smelly slime from the sewer. And secondly, Sally hated me!

I glanced at my watch. It was eight-thirty.

Yikes! Only thirty minutes left!

That's it, I decided. I had no choice.

I'm going in. I slunk up the steps of *The Daily Rat* and squeezed through the doors. I DID IT! I was in! I was so proud of myself I barely noticed where I was going. Before I knew it, I was standing right outside Sally's office.

I peeked inside. Sally was seated behind her huge CRYSTAL desk. The desk was empty except for one thing. I gulped. It was the envelope. The envelope with the **red seal**.

I was just about to dash in and grab it when Sally spotted me. Or should I say smelled me.

"*Geronimo Stilton!*" she screeched.

"**What** are you doing here in my office? You smell worse than the inside of the Cheddartown stables." Just then, she realized I was staring at the envelope.

"Hmm, I see I have something you want," she cackled. She picked up the envelope and **fanned** her snout. "I don't know what it is, but it's mine, mine, mine!"

I groaned. I should have known Sally would never give up without a fight. I tried every trick in the book.

"*FIRE*! ALIENS! Run for your life!" I squeaked. But Sally didn't budge.

Then I had an idea. "Sally, I hate to alarm you," I whispered. "But you broke a pawnail."

That did it. Sally flew into a frenzy. "Where, where?" she shrieked.

In a flash, I grabbed the envelope. I raced for the door.

But I wasn't fast enough. **Sally grabbed me by the tail.** The envelope flew out of my paws. I watched in horror as it drifted out the window.

I felt my heart sink. This was it. I'd never find that envelope again. I was a **dead rat**. And maybe sooner than I thought. Sally's muscular bodyguard was staring at me like I was a piping-hot three-cheese pizza!

"Musclerat, please take Mr. Stilton away. And make sure you teach him a lesson he'll never forget," she ordered with an evil smirk.

Musclerat lifted me into the air with one paw. **HOLEY CHEESE**, that rodent was strong! I mean, I'm not the heaviest mouse in the world, but I'm no lightweight. Plus, I have to admit lately I'd been cheating on my **diet**.

Musclerat **CARRIED** me down the hall. Then he locked me inside the broom closet.

"I heard you liked dark places," he snickered.

I FELT DIZZY. My paws started to sweat. My heart started to pound. I began to sob *uncontrollably*. "Somebody help me," I wailed.

Suddenly, I heard a *click* and the door opened. I felt SOMEONE grab my shoulder.

A deep voice said, *"I'm here to help."*

The same delicate perfume I had smelled before filled my nose.

I tried to say thanks, but I couldn't. I had fainted.

THE CASE OF THE MYSTERIOUS RESCUER

When I came to, I found myself outside. I was sitting on the sidewalk in front of *The Daily Rat*. It was 8:45. I looked all around me, but I didn't see **anyone**.

Who had saved me?

Why did he disappear?

Who had saved me and why?

I felt like I was on one of those true-life **MYSTERY** shows on TV: *The Case of the Mysterious Rescuer.* Too bad, everything wasn't going to work out perfectly in the end. I still hadn't found the lost envelope with the **red seal**. I stared at the ground feeling glum.

My grandfather would never let me live this one down. I'd be *humiliated* in front of all of my coworkers. I'd have to leave the *Gazette*. I'd have no money, **NO JOB**. I'd wander the streets looking for food. Well, at least I knew how to get to the **town dump**. Maybe I could find some scraps of moldy cheese.

A tear slid down my fur. Then another and another. Soon, I was bawling my eyes out. Just then I felt someone touch my shoulder. At the same time, I smelled that perfume again.

"I'm here to help," a deep voice said. And then it hit me. No, not more **garbage**. Not more seagull poop. It hit me who the voice belonged to. I jumped off the curb and whirled around. I was right!

The voice belonged to my old friend, **KORNELIUS**. Yep, I was snout to snout with **OOK** and the fascinating **OOV**!

"How can we help you?" they asked.

I let out a long sigh.

"I lost an envelope, a very important

envelope," I moaned. "And now my grandfather's going to kill me!"

For some reason, **KORNELIUS**, aka **OOK** and his sister, *Veronica*, aka **OOV**, looked at each other and smiled.

"A large envelope?" said OOK. "With a **red seal**?" said OOV.

My jaw hit the ground. These **SECRET AGENTS** were unbelievable!

I had no idea they were mind readers.

I nodded, awestruck. Then Kornelius handed me something. My eyes nearly popped out of my fur.

 **ITWASTHE ENVELOPE!**

"But . . . how . . . when . . . what?" I spluttered.

KORNELIUS just grinned. "We secret agents work in mysterious ways," he said.

His sister, **OOV**, nodded.

I wondered if they could read my mind now. I was so happy. I felt like I had just won a lifetime supply of Cheesy Chews!

Countdown, Five, Four, Three . . .

Suddenly, I remembered the time. I glanced at my paw watch. Holey cheddar chunks! It was **EIGHT FIFTY-FIVE A.M.!**

I only had five minutes to get the envelope to my grandfather.

I took off as fast as my paws could carry me. I was a mouse on a mission — a mission **to save my tail**! I flew up the steps to *The Gazette*, *RACED* past my office, and headed straight for the conference room. By the time I reached the door, I was sweating like an overweight rat on a **TREADMILL**. My paws were aching. And my heart was beating so hard, I thought it might pop right out of my *fur*.

I flung open the door to the conference room just as the clock chimed nine. I wasn't surprised to see my grandfather waiting for me. Did I mention he's a stickler for punctuality?

"Here it is, Grandfather," I huffed, waving the envelope in the air. Then I collapsed in a heap.

"Well, well, well, Grandson. I wasn't sure you had it in you," my grandfather smirked. "But it looks like you passed my test with *flying colors*. You see, Geronimo, the envelope you have contains a **COPY** of the original document. I've had the original **HERE** with me this whole time. I just

wanted to see how much *The Rodent's Gazette* meant to you. And now I can see, it means a lot."

I didn't know whether to *laugh* or cry. But it didn't matter. I had already fainted.

A True Friend . . .

They took me home on a stretcher.

I was exhausted. I slept all day and all night for twenty-four hours straight.

The next day, **OOK** came to see me at the office.

I told him how silly I felt.

"I should have admitted that I needed your help," I **confessed**. "But there's one thing I still don't understand. What made you follow me even after I told you I could take care of myself?"

KORNELIUS laughed. "We secret agents have a sixth sense, Geronimo." He **WINKED**. "Plus, you always had a knack for getting yourself into TROUBLE when we were little. Remember the time you accidentally flew off that **swing** at recess?"

How could I forget? I got stuck in a humongous sticker bush. Youch! My fur hurt just thinking about it.

Before **KORNELIUS** left, he gave me a present. It was a **SPECIAL SATELLITE PHONE** to wear around my neck.

Now all I had to do was press a button to contact my **friend**.

I told you my aunt Sweetfur was right.

Want to read my next adventure?
It's sure to be a fur-raising experience!

A Very Merry Christmas

'Tis the season to be jolly! And holey cheese was I trying...but on my way to New York City to meet my family for the holidays, my luggage got switched with another mouse's! Oh, rats! Now I had to scurry all over the Big Apple trying to find that other mouse and all my presents!

And don't miss any of my other fabumouse adventures!

#1 Lost Treasure of the Emerald Eye

#2 The Curse of the Cheese Pyramid

#3 Cat and Mouse in a Haunted House

#4 I'm Too Fond of My Fur!

#5 Four Mice Deep in the Jungle

#6 Paws Off, Cheddarface!

#7 Red Pizzas for a Blue Count

#8 Attack of the Bandit Cats

#9 A Fabumouse Vacation for Geronimo

#10 All Because of a Cup of Coffee

#11 It's Halloween, You 'Fraidy Mouse!

#12 Merry Christmas, Geronimo!

#13 The Phantom of the Subway

#14 The Temple of the Ruby of Fire

#15 The Mona Mousa Code

#16 A Cheese-Colored Camper

#17 Watch Your Whiskers, Stilton!

#18 Shipwreck on the Pirate Islands

#19 My Name Is Stilton, Geronimo Stilton

#20 Surf's Up, Geronimo!

#21 The Wild, Wild West

#22 The Secret of Cacklefur Castle

A Christmas Tale

#23 Valentine's Day Disaster

**#24 Field Trip to
Niagara Falls**

**#25 The Search for
Sunken Treasure**

**#26 The Mummy
with No Name**

**#27 The Christmas
Toy Factory**

**#28 Wedding
Crasher**

**#29 Down and Out
Down Under**

**#30 The Mouse
Island Marathon**

**#31 The Mysterious
Cheese Thief**

and coming soon

**Christmas
Catastrophe**

**#32 Valley of the
Giant Skeletons**

**#33 Geronimo
and the Gold
Medal Mystery**

**#35 A Very
Merry Christmas**

ABOUT THE AUTHOR

Born in New Mouse City, Mouse Island, Geronimo Stilton is Rattus Emeritus of Mousomorphic Literature and of Neo-Ratonic Comparative Philosophy. For the past twenty years, he has been running *The Rodent's Gazette,* New Mouse City's most widely read daily newspaper.

Stilton was awarded the Ratitzer Prize for his scoops on *The Curse of the Cheese Pyramid* and *The Search for Sunken Treasure.* He has also received the Andersen 2000 Prize for Personality of the Year. One of his bestsellers won the 2002 eBook Award for world's best ratlings' electronic book. His works have been published all over the globe.

In his spare time, Mr. Stilton collects antique cheese rinds and plays golf. But what he most enjoys is telling stories to his nephew Benjamin.

THE RODENT'S GAZETTE

1. **Main entrance**
2. **Printing presses (where the books and newspaper are printed)**
3. **Accounts department**
4. **Editorial room (where the editors, illustrators, and designers work)**
5. **Geronimo Stilton's office**
6. **Storage space for Geronimo's books**

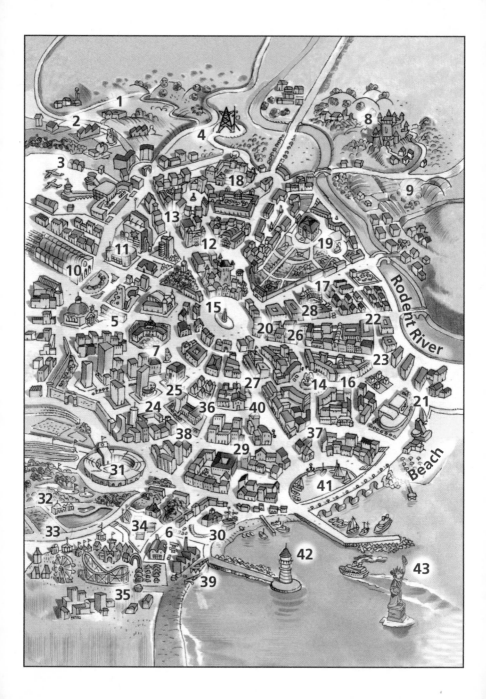

Map of New Mouse City

1. Industrial Zone
2. Cheese Factories
3. Angorat International Airport
4. WRAT Radio and Television Station
5. Cheese Market
6. Fish Market
7. Town Hall
8. Snotnose Castle
9. The Seven Hills of Mouse Island
10. Mouse Central Station
11. Trade Center
12. Movie Theater
13. Gym
14. Catnegie Hall
15. Singing Stone Plaza
16. The Gouda Theater
17. Grand Hotel
18. Mouse General Hospital
19. Botanical Gardens
20. Cheap Junk for Less (Trap's store)
21. Parking Lot
22. Mouseum of Modern Art
23. University and Library
24. *The Daily Rat*
25. *The Rodent's Gazette*
26. Trap's House
27. Fashion District
28. The Mouse House Restaurant
29. Environmental Protection Center
30. Harbor Office
31. Mousidon Square Garden
32. Golf Course
33. Swimming Pool
34. Blushing Meadow Tennis Courts
35. Curlyfur Island Amusement Park
36. Geronimo's House
37. New Mouse City Historic District
38. Public Library
39. Shipyard
40. Thea's House
41. New Mouse Harbor
42. Luna Lighthouse
43. The Statue of Liberty

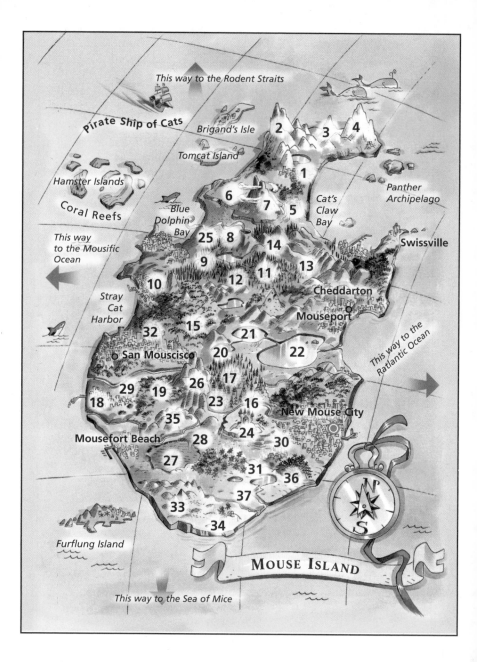

This way to the Rodent Straits

Pirate Ship of Cats

Brigand's Isle

Tomcat Island

Hamster Islands

Coral Reefs

This way
to the Mousific
Ocean

Blue
Dolphin
Bay

Stray
Cat
Harbor

Cat's
Claw
Bay

Panther
Archipelago

Swissville

Cheddarton

Mouseport

This way to the
Ratlantic Ocean

San Mouscisco

New Mouse City

Mousefort Beach

Furflung Island

This way to the Sea of Mice

MOUSE ISLAND

1 2 3 4 5 6 7 8 9 10 11 12 13 14 15 16 17 18 19 20 21 22 23 24 25 26 27 28 29 30 31 32 33 34 35 36 37